W9-BMQ-041

Cowgirl Katie

by Fran Manushkin

illustrated by Tammie Lyon

PICTURE WINDOW BOOKS
a capstone imprint

Katie Woo is published by Picture Window Books
a Capstone Imprint
1710 Roe Crest Drive
North Mankato, Minnesota 56003
www.capstonepub.com

Text © 2014 Fran Manushkin
Illustrations © 2014 Picture Window Books

All rights reserved. No part of this publication may be reproduced in whole or in part, or stored in a retrieval system, or transmitted in any form or by any means, electronic, mechanical, photocopying, recording, or otherwise, without written permission of the publisher.

Library of Congress Cataloging-in-Publication Data
Manushkin, Fran, author.
  Cowgirl Katie / by Fran Manushkin; illustrated by Tammie Lyon.
    pages cm. — (Katie Woo)
  Summary: Katie's dad surprises her with a trip to a ranch where she can ride a real horse.
  ISBN 978-1-4795-2174-6 (library binding)
  ISBN 978-1-4795-2353-5 (paperback)
1. Horses—Juvenile fiction. 2. Cowgirls—Juvenile fiction. 3. Chinese Americans—Juvenile fiction. [1. Horses—Fiction. 2. Cowgirls—Fiction. 3. Chinese Americans—Fiction.] I. Lyon, Tammie, illustrator. II. Title. III. Series: Manushkin, Fran. Katie Woo.
  PZ7.M3195Co 2014
  [E]—dc23   2013028500

Art Director: Kay Fraser
Graphic Designer: Kristi Carlson

Photo Credits:
Greg Holch, pg. 26
Tammie Lyon, pg. 26

Printed in the United States of America.
030520
003316

Table of Contents

Chapter 1
Horse Crazy

Katie was reading about cowgirls. They looked so happy on their horses.

"Yippie-yi-yo!" Katie sang. "Riding a horse looks cool!"

"Guess what I want for my birthday?" said Katie. "A horse! I'll feed him carrots and ride him in the yard."

"Our yard is too small," said Katie's mom. "Horses need a field, and they cost a lot of money."

"I have money in my piggy bank," said Katie.

But it was not enough.

Katie told JoJo, "If I had a horse, I'd ride as fast as the wind!"

"Horses are big," said JoJo. "I might be afraid to ride one."

"Not me," said Katie.

Katie wrote a poem in her journal:

"I want a horse!

I do! Of course.

I'd ride it all day,

Up, up, and away!"

Katie pretended her bike
was a horse.

"Giddy-up!" she shouted.

But her bike didn't have a
mane and a tail.

Katie rode a horse on the merry-go-round.

"Giddy-up!" she yelled.

The horse had a mane and a tail, but they were made of wood.

Katie collected horse stickers and put them everywhere.

Pedro teased her, "You are horse crazy."

"You bet!" said Katie.

Chapter 2
A Ranch Trip

One day, Katie's dad said,
"I have a surprise. I am taking
you to a ranch."

"Will I ride a horse?" asked
Katie.

"Yes!" said her dad. "JoJo
and Pedro are coming too."

They got into their van

and rode to the ranch.

"Hello, horses!" Katie

yelled. "Wow! You sure are

big!"

Pedro and JoJo got on their horses. But Katie said, "Wait! First I want to give my horse a carrot."

The horse liked the carrot. He nuzzled Katie with his big head.

"Come on!" yelled JoJo.

"Get on your horse and ride

with us!"

"I better not," said Katie.

"My horse looks tired. He

wants to rest."

"Katie," said her mom, "when I was little, I was scared of horses."

"You were?" said Katie. "I'm a little worried. My horse is so high up."

"He is," said Katie's dad.

"But I'll be holding on to

you."

"You will?" said Katie.

"That would be great!"

Chapter 3
Ride 'Em, Katie!

Katie got on the horse.

"Whoo!" Katie said. "Here I go!"

Her horse began walking slowly.

"Let's go faster," said Katie. So the horse began trotting!

"Ride 'em, cowgirl!" Pedro
yelled.

"I'm riding!" shouted
Katie. "I'm riding!"

Katie sang a cowgirl song:

"I like this horse.

I do! Of course!

I could ride all day!

Yippee-yi-yo! Hurray!"

After the ride, Katie gave
her horse a hug and said,
"Thank you! I'll never forget
you."

"Katie," said her mom, "you were very brave."

"I know," said Katie. "I'm a cowgirl. We are always brave — most of the time!"

About the Author

Fran Manushkin is the author of many popular picture books, including *Baby, Come Out!*; *Latkes and Applesauce: A Hanukkah Story*; *The Tushy Book*; *The Belly Book*; and *Big Girl Panties*. There is a real Katie Woo — she's Fran's great-niece — but she never gets in half the trouble of the Katie Woo in the books. Fran writes on her beloved Mac computer in New York City, without the help of her two naughty cats, Chaim and Goldy.

About the Illustrator

Tammie Lyon began her love for drawing at a young age while sitting at the kitchen table with her dad. She continued her love of art and eventually attended the Columbus College of Art and Design, where she earned a bachelors degree in fine art. After a brief career as a professional ballet dancer, she decided to devote herself full time to illustration. Today she lives with her husband, Lee, in Cincinnati, Ohio. Her dogs, Gus and Dudley, keep her company as she works in her studio.

Glossary

crazy (KRAY-zee)—very enthusiastic

journal (JUR-nuhl)—a diary in which you regularly write down your thoughts and experiences

merry-go-round (MER-ee-goh-round)—a revolving platform for riding at amusement parks and fairs, often with seats in the form of horses or other animals

nuzzled (NUHZ-uhld)—cuddled

poem (POH-uhm)—a piece of writing set in short lines, often with a rhythm and words that rhyme

ranch (RANCH)—a large farm for cattle, sheep, or horses

trotting (TROT-teeng)—moving slightly faster than a walking pace

Discussion Questions

1. Katie's dad surprised her with a trip to a ranch. It was a wonderful surprise! Talk about a time when you got a nice surprise.

2. Katie is crazy about horses. What are you crazy about?

3. Katie felt nervous about riding the horse, but her parents made her feel better. How do your parents make you feel better when you are nervous or unhappy?

Writing Prompts

1. Write down three facts about horses. If you can't think of three, ask a grown-up to help you find some in a book or on the computer.

2. Imagine what a horse ranch is like. What things do you see there? What does it smell like? What sounds do you hear? Write a paragraph describing what you imagine.

3. Katie wrote a poem about horses. Write your own poem about something you love.

Horseback riding works up an appetite! This boot-shaped sandwich is the perfect snack after a day on a ranch. Ask a grown-up for help and don't forget to wash your hands!

Boot-and-Spur Sammie

Ingredients:

- Two pieces of wheat bread
- Peanut butter
- Fruit strip

Other things you need:

- butter knife
- kitchen scissors
- boot-shaped cookie cutter (optional)
- small star-shaped cookie cutter (optional)

What you do:

1. With the butter knife, make a peanut-butter sandwich with the two pieces of bread.

2. Using the butter knife (rinse it off first) or a boot-shaped cookie cutter, cut out a boot from the sandwich. (You can eat the outside parts, too, so just set those to the side.)

3. Using the kitchen scissors, cut six small triangles from your fruit strip. Line them up along the outside of the boot, three on each side, to make a pattern, as in the picture.

4. Using either a star-shaped cookie cutter or the kitchen scissors, cut a star from the fruit strip. Connect the star to the boot using a bit of crust from the outside part of the sandwich.

You can add jelly in your sandwich if you prefer PB&J. Serve with a tall glass of milk for a real cowgirl treat!

THE FUN DOESN'T STOP HERE!

Discover more at www.capstonekids.com

- Videos & Contests
- Games & Puzzles
- Friends & Favorites
- Authors & Illustrators

Find cool websites and more books like this one at www.facthound.com. Just type in the Book ID: **9781479521746** and you're ready to go!